GRASSROOTS
Rhythmic Travels of the Soul

Sean P. Tyler

Copyright © 2003 by Sean P. Tyler

All rights reserved. No part of this book shall be reproduced or transmitted in any form or by any means, electronic, mechanical, magnetic, photographic including photocopying, recording or by any information storage and retrieval system, without prior written permission of the publisher. No patent liability is assumed with respect to the use of the information contained herein. Although every precaution has been taken in the preparation of this book, the publisher and author assume no responsibility for errors or omissions. Neither is any liability assumed for damages resulting from the use of the information contained herein.

ISBN 0-7414-1740-5

Published by:

INFINITY
PUBLISHING.COM

1094 New Dehaven Street
Suite 100
West Conshohocken, PA 19428-2713
Info@buybooksontheweb.com
www.buybooksontheweb.com
Toll-free (877) BUY BOOK
Local Phone (610) 941-9999
Fax (610) 941-9959

Printed in the United States of America

Printed on Recycled Paper

Published May 2004

GRASSROOTS RHYTHMIC TRAVELS OF THE SOUL

Table of Contents

1. WELCOME TO MY WORDZ 1
2. WHEN STARS WISH ON US 3
3. SPIRITUALITY (WHAT I BELIEVE) 5
4. BLACK BIRDS 7
5. A NEW AARON AND MOSES 9
6. ANGEL BY MY SIDE 11
7. KISSES IN A BOTTLE 13
8. I KNOW 15
9. WITHOUT YOU 19
10. PHENOMENAL BROTHER 21
11. GRASSROOTS PART I (REFLECTIONS) 23
12. UNFAITHFUL 27
13. SEAN'S DEFINITION OF A POET 29
14. 100 PROOF YOU 32
15. A WORK OF A.R.T 35
16. LIKE A TATTOO 39
17. I SEE THROUGH TEARS 41
18. AIN'T NOBODY LIKE ME (FLAWS AND ALL) 43
19. BACK TO REALITY 45
20. TRIBUTE 47
21. SWEET SLAVERY 49
22. WHY DO I WRITE? 51
23. IN THE DARK 53
24. LOVE INTOXICATION 55
25. REAL INTIMACY 59
26. EXHIBIT A 61
27. GRASSROOTS PART II (DEEPLY ROOTED) 65
28. WE!!! HE??? 71
29. BOYS LIKE ME 73
30. EYES OF AN ANGEL 75
31. GRANDMAW'S HANDS 77
32. CONQUERABLE SOUL 79
33. A MACK GONE GOOD (SEAN'S REFORMATION) 81
34. IF YOU CAN COUNT YOUR MONEY 83
35. BETWEEN THE NUMBERED SHEETS 87
36. SIMPLE COMPLEXITY 89
37. NO ONE 91
38. MOURNING DEW 93
39. HOW GOOD INTENTIONS DIE 95
40. WEDDING DAY BLISS 97
41. THE CALM AFTER MY STORMS (ME AT 35) 99

GRASSROOTS
Rhythmic Travels of the Soul

To contact the author for readings, comments or interviews please do so at www.Grassroots777@aol.com

GRASSROOTS
Rhythmic Travels of the Soul

WELCOME TO MY WORDZ

My words have started mental revolutions
and at times calmed my spirit's seas
In written form they burn through pages
when spoken
they save forest trees

My words create a renaissance each day
they take the focus from
the gifts you give
to the gifts you say
a sort of
verbal bouquet

My words flow from the speaker into a speaker
while on center stage
a self-discovery gauge
they never seek accolades
but
are award-worthy each page

My words know no limit
on your heart they get inscripted
deliberate
truth is truth
regardless of
what religious or spiritual name you give it
it's simplistic
open your mind
it's your growing time
when My Wordz come to visit

GRASSROOTS
Rhythmic Travels of the Soul

WHEN STARS WISH ON US

Majestic plus excellent
Your beauty is off the curve scale
You set a whole new precedent
Your words are my heart's testament
Our chemistry
Is beyond any
"Once upon a time..." infamy
Intensely, we
Elevate instinctively,
And I love how your body clings to me
Indeed you read my needs
And then your spirit sings to me
The originals called it "heaven"
And that's, what you bring to me
No lie
With a closed eye, I
Feel as if I, can see the most high
No x-tasy to get me high
Your touch
Is my rush
Your kiss, is beyond
Any tight-eyed kid's birthday wish
And then I get a little dizzy
Almost tipsy
And let's just say
It's
As good as it gets!

Makes me forget who I am
Due to my mantra being your name
Thought I was a mack
But you took all of that
So if the truth be told
I got, got
Because you got game
All the same
You still let me be king of the jungle
But now I'm humble and tamed

A pleasant surprise
A blessing in disguise
Want to continue to give you blue skies
So I'm learning compromise
Holistic love on the rise
So we can tie a double knot
In our family ties
Besides,
When you get a thought
I want to become its equivalent action
Not 50/50
At times you need more from me
Anyway, since when did
Entirely complimenting love become a fraction?
I'm here to add helium to your dreams
And purpose to your passions
No subtractions
Eternal times everlasting

No clouds
I can see destiny for miles
And true love removes fears
During our journey our milestones
Will be called years
And since "Men are from Mars"
I may not always make sense
But,
I will always be sincere

No fight, no fuss
Just
Truth and trust,
Go from making wishes
To having stars, wish on us

SPIRITUALITY (WHAT I BELIEVE)

I believe in
What I can't see
It's what supports wings
Resurrects trees
It's both the hedge and the haven
The source watching over me
It's in the make up
Of everything that we can see
Even though we
Can't see what it is truly
I believe

Deeper than my DNA
It hears my heart
When I forget to pray
Allows good memories to linger
Even when they occurred
More than 20 years worth of yesterdays

It keeps us while we are asleep
It's beyond distant galaxies
While at the same time
Closer than your next heartbeat
Makes oceans and seas seem shallow
Because...
It's so deep

It fills in gaps
Overlaps
But can't be located on maps

It's language is universal
And it's laws are respected
Karma with compassion
When it's motions are harnessed
We call it electric
The pause in the song
The gap from second to second
It is the space in between EVERYTHING

Earthly isolation
Makes it appear we're separate
But we call it love once we realize
We are supremely connected

It escorts your grandparents home
When they last close their eyes
And whispers their words of wisdom to you
In order to guide your
And others' lives

It's both Mother Nature
And Father Time
It's Mary's sacrificial lamb
In that nursery rhyme

It is the Ancient Of Days
Before numerical years
The tamer of Egos
The opposite of fears

It's beyond the five senses
Not pretentious
Compliments us
Our life's story
Every sentence
And that's, what I Believe

BLACK BIRDS

His wings must be heavy
in this rain
will he cease to sing
or maybe
unknowingly to me
he chirps to complain
My burdened dreams
which once too had wings
now seem damp and in vain
And when my gloom seems to loom
I go to the nest in my room
to get out of
the pouring pain

GRASSROOTS
Rhythmic Travels of the Soul

A NEW AARON AND MOSES (AHMAD AND SEAN)

Somewhere west of Galilee
You can find me S.T.
And little A-H-M-A-D
Walking a city street
With modern sandals called
Iverson's and Air Jordan's
On our feet
A new Aaron and Moses
Traded in our staffs
For inkpads crayons and book bags
Which proves to be
Superior weaponry
To technologies of the enemy
So when we throw down lyrically
You can see
It swallows
The snakes from the beast
Going internal
To get to eternal peace
Blessings never cease
With Ahmad my sun
My woman Angel my moon
Our unborn children are stars
Myself and my God make my cipher complete
A circle of unity- 360
And since there's no Red Sea that I can see
We will not run from the enemy
Because the Million that I Marched with
And the 143,998 we represent
Believe gods don't retreat

GRASSROOTS
Rhythmic Travels of the Soul

ANGEL BY MY SIDE

The softest of kisses
the fulfillment of dreams now true
the answer to
life anew
silent prayers and my unasked wishes

My Angel that has always been
my enchanting lover
my future children's mother
and currently- my best friend

By my side
she's heaven exemplified
even by myself I am never alone
she's the sum total
of all the good I've known
love full blown
my heart is her home
more than the net worth
a billionaire times ten could own
allowed to reap
more than I have sown
even in our absent times
through our connected hearts
and telekinetic minds
we have continually grown

She represents the smile of a new season
and seemingly loves without needing a reason
her beauty carries like a saxophone note
with the eye pleasing flair of a paintbrush stroke

She is the genesis of my happiness
intelligence, plus passion, plus elegance
both Alpha and "infinance"
nurturing life in between
My compass
My queen
My soul-mate, My life-mate

both my reality
and a wide awake dream
elevates me to heights unseen
given the name Angel
because
in a word
she is
Supreme

KISSES IN A BOTTLE

Your words are like
kisses
to my ears
they
stimulate my mind
and sometimes
I feel as if
you've
found a secret way to
fondle me
on the inside

I try to look away and deny
and when you ask
"what's wrong"
I reply
"nothing I'm just face shy"
knowing that if I look up
I will lock on to your eyes
lose my train of thought
slur my speech
and become
momentarily
physically
paralyzed
the truth needs no support
and my words know no lies
I'm in awe everyday
while hourly being pleasantly surprised

The least I could do is to be true
devote my life
and slay modern dragons
for you
and one by one eliminate your fears
my peers
look for love inside of clubs
because they are publicly searching
for what we have privately found

in our sacred space here
And
I feel blessed beyond any man
with you giving me
more than I could ever want
while encouraging me to be
more of who I am
which is your lover and friend
a strong and sincere individual
but face to face with you
I tend to
melt
and give in
when
you say those sweet things
that you say
I want to put your words in a bottle
and slowly sip from them...all day

I KNOW

I can remember my proud brother
who served in Vietnam
come home only to
be called a "nigger"
while still in uniform

I know about having a best friend expire
from gun fire
and statistically
I know my life expectancy
is the same age
as when I should retire

I know the hallway stench
in hi-rise/low income
buildings
looked into the sunken eyes
of crack babies and held
chemically dependant children

I know how to stretch 10 dollars
until the first of the month
I know about dinners consisting of
expired milk and Captain Crunch

cold showers
cemetery flowers
no lights, no cable
so we climbed the pole to restore
the power
used my sisters name
to turn on my phone
for heat I had to sleep
breathing warm breaths
under the covers
with my clothes still on

I know about dreams deferred
and promises unkept

seen precious daughters use the title "daddy"
for the last jobless man
with whom their mother slept

I know vision cards, cell bars
gang wars, stolen cars
no recess just juvenile jail yards

abortion clinics
the crack epidemic
drive- bys, hungry baby cries
alley ways where a "john" pays
and African queens' open thighs
400 years of Willie Lynch based lies

I have been the subject
of dumb racial jokes
seen a crying teen
holding braided shoestrings
and read their suicide notes

I know about wrongful drug convictions
house arrests and house evictions
seen broken homes
lead to confusion and friction
misery loves drugs
and kind words are rarely louder
than the voice of someone's addiction
slavery is the same
plantation or prison
youth advisor
was my description
they had no room for hope
they were full of dope
in the form of Buspar, Zoloft and Ridolin

I have seen HIV ladies
pass it on to
their sweet innocent
butterscotch babies

I know sisters
who give all of their purse
to the collection at church
living off of prayer
and air sandwiches until the first
so what's worse...
blessed and hungry
or paid and cursed?
politicians and preachers lie
that's why
we suffer
because the absence of truth hurts
so why vote democrat or republican
when it's the system that doesn't work

I have seen welfare
say farewell to good intending men
allowing women to become complacent
have children who start that
same cycle again

I know about being under-represented and over-taxed
while our public school needs new books
teaching children that
being robbed by officials of education
is a prerequisite
to later understanding corporate crooks

I know girls who sell
what's illegal
before they are legal
so tell me how does a boy in the inner city
get a hold of a gun
called Desert Eagle

I have seen men hide behind sex
but unable to give
their children hugs
I've known once good mothers
loan their esteem to processed bad foods
and harmful weight loss drugs

I know skinny women
who were once hourglasses...
closed caskets

I have seen
many things
but still I strive
because
I see the promise of tomorrow
when I see my
son's eyes

WITHOUT YOU (MY SILENT CONFESSION)

I can't sleep
Haven't washed dishes in a week
I retreat
To memories left in the same perfumed sheets...
My Life Stinks

No shadow in the dark
Rhythmless heart
Eyes without spark
My fateless end, her fresh start

Personal recession
My possessions lessen
Cursed my blessin'
Decompose, depression
This is, my silent confession

Thin air
Holds nothing in which you can believe
No desires
One need
Be still and heal
Maturity hates greed
No confrontation
Without congregation
How can I lead

Carbon copy
Of my body
But sloppy
Heard pills kill
So Love, please stop me
Lead me in the direction
Of still waters and affection

Need you to soothe me
Dereliction of duty
Leaves me no one to hold
But told

To "get a grip"
I drowned in love
You abandoned ship
I planted seeds of good deeds
But my needs
Were never met
I'll forgive if
You'll regret
You choose
"No thank you's"
I'm confused
You're amused
And can't see we both lose
As quiet as kept

I would chew on the letters
And digest the E-mails you would send me
But now I grow skinny
No drugs just
Lack of nutrition and intimacy
I need a rehab for co-dependency
Do you think of me?
Will you at least remember me?
My confused mind
Saves memories
That I've tried to delete
I reach for my deodorant
To brush my teeth
Dial your number
But unable to speak
And remember to forget
I am nothing without you
And you, are better
Without me

PHENOMENAL BROTHER (For Maya)

Look at Me,
being the man my ancestors
wanted me to be,
attacking those fears
that once shackled me,
strong backboned, "melanated" skin tone,
I'm a man, phenomenally.
Phenomenal brother, that's me.

I've had my three-day stay
and under dreads, fades and bald heads
my mind arose
on a sweet path to perfection, going for more
than just some reparations someone owes.

No stereotype can define me.
No linear thinking can explain
how I wrap myself in my royal ancestral greatness,
proudly wearing my fathers and mothers names.
They were phenomenal to me,
so I am their phenomenal son,
spiritually and physically,
with phenomenal blood in me.

Through the toil and tears, I persist.
The memories are not forgotten.
With dark rich soil, covering my strong roots,
my family tree brought forth fruit like me.
No matter who "can not tell a lie," then does,
or, continues to keep on chopping.

Out of love for the woman
who put the X chromosome in me
I seek to repay another deservedly
by being a lover, respecter, helper and protector daily.
I call them phenomenal,
and in turn, they also honor me.

I marched with a million brothers

and hugged all I could.
I have no intentions to stop
because I'm getting high
off of doing good.

I've got a kind word for my people,
regardless of their position,
because I know, "United We Grow"
and the spirit can do for you as it did for me,
and touch any condition.
Consciously, I strive fervently
to be, your phenomenal brother, proudly.
I am a loving black man - father and friend
representing wonderfully
Phenomenal Me.

GRASSROOTS PART I (Reflections)

To all my people
who can remember getting commodities
on 5th street...
that government cheese sure is the best,
ain't it?
You make up the grassroots.

To all of my "sistas" who know
$50 worth of food stamps
will bring $25 cash,
because "I'm not going to miss that concert."

The grassroots are the "brothas"
who gave 5 on the backhand side,
then in the hole,
fluffed your fro,
cause you got soul.
The grassroots used to "say it loud,"
and now, wonder why the youth ain't even
thinkin' it soft or low.
"Sistas" singin', "R-E-S-P-E-C-T"
men sayin', "dig this." "I dug that." "Can you dig it?",
and "What's up Bro?"
Wishin' you Love, Peace and Soul
cause once a week
the Grassroots were all tryin'
to catch the Soooullll - Train.

We put our women on pedestals,
and our children on knee ponies
after working on
not trying to work hard
all week.

Our silky, untrained voices
belt out Smokey's and Marvin's greatest
we singing to music that was dubbed
from a tape
that was borrowed from a friend's mother's

uncle's sister's cousin.

Slam! Dominoes in barbershops. Bam!
"Give me 20 stitches in yo' britches."
Bam! "Follow that cab."
Bam! "I'll take a dime 'cause tennis shoes
make yo' feet hurt."
Bam! "I domino. Shake 'em Jake cause
my fingers ache."

Here's to my people who keep that 'Du' tight
and can make a 'Du-Rag' from
a panty hose stocking, pillow case or handkerchief.

The Grassroots write checks on Wednesdays
knowing that we don't get paid until Fridays.
We are the ones to be watched
because if left alone,
we become heavyweight boxing champions
in 90 seconds,
moonwalk, spin around 5 times,
stop, land on the tip of our toenails, and
throw up a white gloved hand
while the other hand
signs a billion dollar contract with Sony.

We must again realize we are the Supremes,
and as important as the elements,
Earth, Wind and Fire,
Today we're the groups with Tender Lovin' Care (TLC).
We are forever B.I.G., Boys 2 (or becoming) Men, Black
Star, Common Sense, Ja Rule
H to the O, V to the A (HOVA), The Roots, Mary Mary,
Destiny's Child, God's Son and yet still remain the Public's
Enemy.
The Grassroots went on what would normally be
suicide missions, and landed safely in Tuskegee
without a bruise.

We would throw a "Rent Party" on the last Friday of the
month

and occasionally "borrow" the change from Grand-Dad's sock
to play "The Numbers"

We marched beside and behind King and Malcolm
and although they are Giants,
It is our baby steps that continue to move us forward.
Things don't change until We
say, "Revolution."
The Grassroots become
the world's best Doctors, Lawyers, Mechanics, Writers, Teachers,
Mothers, Fathers, Scientists, Sociologists, Entertainers and Poets
and still, take the time out to say
"No sir" and "Yes Ma'am".

GRASSROOTS
Rhythmic Travels of the Soul

UNFAITHFUL

I made love with my pen
and then
promised to spend
time with it each day
I guess
the union was blessed
but I'll be the first to say
I cheated
found other outlets
to emotionally sleep with
formed nonwriting habits
that left my creativity depleted
I broke my daily plan
put my hand
on a lesser demand
and
then put my pen beneath it

So forgive me just one more time
please be kind
whether by prose, free verse or rhyme
I always find
my way back to where you are
And to prove that this time
there will be no more cheating or lying
Your jealousy
led me
to key the paint job
on my own car

GRASSROOTS
Rhythmic Travels of the Soul

SEAN'S DEFINITION OF A POET

POET (po·et) -a painter of word pictures, framed by timeless ideas

-a non evasive realist; a totally evasive dreamer

-a highly skilled, and highly selective wordsmith

-one who breathes new life into dormant ears

-a florist of hearts

-a writer of the highest decree

-one who privately delights in the intimacy of language

-one who publicly shares his/her naked lessons

-an illuminated visionary

-one who loans vision to those who are reality-blind

-a master of word grouping and thought spacing

-a spirited deliberator, who allows words to become powerful, explosive, passionate, humble and reflective
causing the receiver to cry, ponder, laugh, smile, dance, and
sashay

-an Artist of the highest calling

-a predetermined, preselected, steward
of a neverending profession

-one who foresees and ushers in a renaissance

-a link to the unexplainable; one who peeks at the invisible;
and details the indescribable

-the twister of narration

-a free thinking, slave of the word

-a spoken word god

-a written word brick mason

-a fashioner of eloquent stanzas, built from simplistic lines

-an elevated servant, who receives inspiration
by living a grounded existence

-one who seeks seclusion and risks being understood,
in order to receive an undiluted understanding

-a watchful vessel

-a seeker for the meaning of yesterday

-a knower of tomorrow

-a lover of NOW

POETS (po·ets) -the only totally free people
   on this planet, so far

GRASSROOTS
Rhythmic Travels of the Soul

100 Proof You

As passion simmers
and my next breath pushes your name
from my lips,
sweet words from you do follow
and from your hive,
the metaphorical honey drips.

I pledge my love.
Then you respond
in the form of the ultimate reply.
You've got a kiss that makes me drunk
and a smile that gets me high.

When I come down,
somewhere between divinity and ecstasy
is where I fall
I'm in need of group therapy
for my addiction to you,
admitting, I can't handle a love withdrawal.

My pleasant addiction
is not due to satin night clothes,
baths laced with petals from a red rose,
or silhouettes from a fireplace.
What's to blame came before
the fine restaurants, chocolates
and dancing to slow tapes.

What is solely responsible,
and no truth serum
could make this more true,
should be measured, bottled, labeled
and called 100 Proof You.

GRASSROOTS
Rhythmic Travels of the Soul

A Work of A.R.T.

He is three
The first branch on my tree
one tenth the age
and half the height of me.
His name is Ahmad Rasoul Tyler
which makes his initials A.R.T.
This is by design
because I love both the art of poetry
and my son
eternally and unequivocally

His mommy, Tammy
kisses his bruised elbows
and the scrapes on his knee,
pours love in his heart
and keeps him smart enough
for Jeopardy,
she placed
a sun-dipped smile on his face
while his granny, Francis
affectionately known as "Cookie"
makes sure that he
stays dressed to a "T".

Ahmad tells me that he
wants to be
the next Michael Jordan, Michael Jackson,
Muhammad Ali and Bruce Lee
so he
jumps and slam dunks
and from his toy box shoots a "three,"
gives me hits
with his padded karate sticks
and flying kicks
to my knee
and then makes me sing back up

to his re-mix of
"A,B,C - 1,2,3, daddy, you and me."

As you can see
he
keeps my
head to the sky
and I "float like a butterfly,"
because he
is as sweet as a honey bee.

When I offer my help,
he says, "I can dude it all by myself,"
stating, "Daddy, I a big boy. I not a baby."
then I reply,
"Well excuse me, Mr. Think-you're-grown-at-three,
Mr. A-H-M-A-D, Mr. A.R.T.,
Mr. I-love-you, you-love-me,
Mr. I'm-scared-of-the-dark, Mr. three-foot-three."

"Mr. coloring-outside-the-lines."
He smiles and it somehow reminds
that creating outside the lines
is only a sign
that he is not conformed to visual confines
which leads me to wonder,
"Is it a sign of success or
a sign on the times
that while I program my computer,
I am being programmed
to use less than ten percent
of my mind?"
Realizing I am
visually and mentally confined
because I was taught to
stay inside the lines.

So see

that is how he,
the most beautiful work of A.R.T.
reminds me of me
when I was three
and more importantly
of a time when I was free.

GRASSROOTS
Rhythmic Travels of the Soul

Like A Tattoo

My heart is hollow.
The words are far out of reach.
Your feelings were shallow.
I thought you belonged to me,
but your purchase
turned out to be a lease.

"Never again," I said
would I fall so deep,
not knowing my reality
was only a temporary dream
that awakening the morning after
would not allow me to keep.

Safe somewhere in your arms
is a place you said I could reside.
No more pain was the promise,
and the promise manifested
when later I realized you had lied.

I will never be able to erase
the life and love
that was shared with you.
I will wear the scars from the memories
they will remain like a tattoo.

A tattoo
that even time
will not be able to completely erase.
A memory,
a precious, permanent memory
of equating forever
with your face.

Your words became my food
and I depended on you
like air.
Your tone turned into a raging storm
when once it was soft and as comforting

as a prayer.

I never believed in any religion
more than I believe in you.
Your heart I would claim
if you would take and keep my name,
and wear it proudly
like a tattoo.

Even as hours turned into weeks
and now I dread the years,
the thoughts bring on sadness
which is the predecessor
to my ever-flowing tears.

My mind dives into a pool of yesterdays
and becomes submerged by the moment
when I wanted to fight for you,
instead of with you.
U-S(us) became V-S(VS)
taking you from being my companion
to my unsuspected opponent.
The promises of tomorrow
are the untruths of today when concerning you,
but even without help I have hope.
So thanks,
for the pain,
tears,
lies,
reality based fears,
and, oh yeah,
most of all
thank you for the tattoo.

I SEE THROUGH TEARS

I see through tears

that linger in my eye sockets

for far too long.

I see through tears

that cloud the possibilities

that are before me.

From hurt, shame and loneliness

my abandoned dreams dissolve.

It is so hard and scary to love again,

trust and commit again,

to see beauty,

and the hope that awaits me

because...

I
  see
     through
         tears.

GRASSROOTS
Rhythmic Travels of the Soul

AIN'T NOBODY LIKE ME (Flaws and All)

I'm unique, from my head to my feet.
THERE'S NOBODY LIKE ME

My soulful style and my crooked smile
leads me to believe there's nobody like me.

Got a Clydesdale strut in my walk,
pride in all I do, while bellowing stereo sounds
when I talk. Nobody even compares to me.

Nose just right for my face.
Perfect lips for when I got a kiss to taste.
No one else - could be me.

Got this handshake with a soul-brother grip.
Got this positive vibe that causes the youth to say
"Aw he's down" and the old timers to say
"Hey that cat is hip." Nobody, No.bo.dy like me.

Sometimes I can change a woman's complexion
making her temperature rise
without a touch or a word,
but with a stare from my pearly black eyes.
My woman said, "Honey - Nobody like you."
"Right baby, there's only one me."

Doing things far beyond others' belief,
I'm that freedom fighter, inventor, sports star
mixed with prophet, king
and indigenous chief

Shoot verbal swords when I talk,
because I too am a scholar, with intellect
and pride that didn't come
from a hairstyle, expensive automobile or a paycheck.
Can we all agree, there's only one me?

I'm just saying I'm in love with myself,
and that's the truth. So, I guess this truth

helps me to be free.
So just understand when you see me celebrating me being me.

BACK TO REALITY (FOR MASTER O.B. KAMAU)

Some days I walk to the window
and feel taller than any building that I see
until I listen to the radio or watch T.V.

I hear things like, "I shot me"
"I stole from myself"
and "I'm a poor unemployed minority"
Then I catch myself and say
"In a world where 8 out of 10 are people of color,
who is the majority?"

It gets so bad that I can't see me
and my hearing, I mean my vision gets blurry
as I try to find myself in history
no I mean his-story

The blood of kings run through me
but in his-story this has never been told
But all the while I'm reminded
of how I was shackled, beat, enslaved and sold

So I hear this for 400 years and alter my goals
and no longer shoot for the stars
I'll settle for the clouds
and my opinions I will keep
or if I voice them it's to myself
and even then it's not loud

So when I get to know myself
maybe I will be myself
rule and school myself, help myself
and then I will want to remember my true self
because I'm tired of being somebody else

Since man came from dirt
and all dirt is either dark red, black or brown
that should be enough proof of my existence
and how long I've been around

I have a future of fortune
spewing from my ancestral well of wealth
though I have named everything on earth
except my black-skinned, white-name-having self

So who is this deceptive dragon
and how do I slay him because surely he must fail
Ah, I will use the sword of economics
packed in a holster of betrayal

Remembering that King's "dream"
of children walking hand in hand
was about the practice of equality in economics, politics
and the respecting of today's black woman and man

So sing it loud "I'm black and I'm proud!
Now sing it right. "O.K. I'm black and I'm unemployed."
"I'm black and I'm a 15-year-old mother,
whose mother is only 15 years older than
her first child,
but it's not so bad.
I have a brother who tells me he's a "rock star"
I never see him with a band
but he sure has a lot of fans,
so I'll keep my head up today and live for tomorrow
and maybe work for my brother
because he gets paid no matter where he's at,
He says his distribution business is "always good"
because "the antidote for despair is crack ."

TRIBUTE

I will chant your name
with each breath
until I die
It alone
is my favorite love song
my
battle cry

My mind's eye
sees you all alone
I build you a house
you make it our home
I give you my seed
your temple receives
and gives back a life
having your bright eyes
with features
mirroring me

Our journey and destiny
are dipped in infinity
our trinity
is what love
was intended to be

Your image is in the back of
a singer's mind
when he births a beautiful song
YOU are why men risk their lives in war
and why I write poems

GRASSROOTS
Rhythmic Travels of the Soul

SWEET SLAVERY

I'm a slave to your love.
Don't want to be emancipated or liberated
from you either.

I want to be tied,
bound,
locked down,
and found
in your control.

I work on a job all day,
come home and house slave.

Pick yo' cotton from the laundry basket,
cook, clean, I mean anything,
You just ask it,

Want to be entertained?
Well then I'll pluck a string and dance a jig,
striptease, "cause I aims ta' please."
I've finished all of my day time chores,
and now you're my night gig.

I'll step and fetch
you a cool drink and have a toast to me and you.
As the night swallows the sun,
servin' you becomes fun.
I'll be much obliged to give you
a kiss so gentle,
that the moon wishes to be human too.

Don't try to trade me for another
and don't worry, I won't try and run.
The slaves of old received 100 lashes for reading.
Today, I read you my poetry,
confessions of freedom coming from this slave's tongue.

Let's jump a broom,
share a crop of young ones,

'cause in you is my emancipation.
A slave to your desires
I forever will be
so keep me
on this Love plantation.

WHY DO I WRITE?

You asked why do I write?
'Cause, Hell, I have to.
It's my therapy, my equalizer.
My pen, has been, my gun, my gin,
an all-understanding and ever-available girlfriend.
I can pick her up at any time, no curfew
or subjects considered taboo.
Give me a page and a pen
and I'll make 50 words into 5 million...pictures.
I write to free myself, to show me myself.
You can take my T.V., my phone, my CD
but don't try to take my notebook from me.
If I had to choose,
it would be a toss up
between
writing and breathing.

GRASSROOTS
Rhythmic Travels of the Soul

IN THE DARK

In the dark, I confront the man
in my mirror,
the one that was on the inside of me
looking out,
in the dark.

In the dark, my house is as big as Bill Gates',
physique more appealing than Denzel's.
I'm a man with power, respected like a prophet,
while in the dark.

I solve world issues, soar through the air
outscoring Kobe,
travel the globe 10 times in my own jet
and get back in my room before breakfast.
I'm a baaad man! - in the dark.

In the dark
I am as free as a daydream.
I save endangered species
like whales, bald eagles, exotic rare birds
and my uncle Harry.

When the morning sunlight shines and daytime comes,
I settle for my so-so job, so-so lifestyle
and I say "I can't help it" and "you know they
won't let us get ahead."
But mainly, it's because I forget who I was
in the dark.

GRASSROOTS
Rhythmic Travels of the Soul

LOVE INTOXICATION (Four Men's Experiences Told As One Story)

After the first sip
I began to stagger and lose the vision I once had.
I immediately put myself second, you first, and
family and friends somewhere on the shelf.
My addiction for you grew quick,
without control or limitations. It wasn't that,
"I'll steal the sun out of the sky for you" love.
It was that real, "I'll get another job for you,
massage your zones, bring all the lovin' and money home to you" love.
I should've noticed the spread of toxins
when all of that and more wasn't enough.
Having minor discussions, about major issues which could
only be addressed between your favorite T.V. shows.
No "thank you's" for house, cars and clothes.
Saying I love you was scarce, so was sex,
as tears dripped from my nose
on to my ink pad.
I even began to think mad.
Called my dad,
and he said, "Son, I too am alone.
Had a sip or two from that intoxicating love stuff you be on."
Called mom and she said,
"Stay son, do it for your kid," so I did.
Thinking her, plus me, plus him
would form a love pyramid and rid
me of the fragmented feelings
a man has after giving his best.
I shared it with a friend I had known
and he shared some other toxins his girl is on.
"No J, No P" is what he told me.
"No justice no peace" I said.
"Naw man." "No Job, No Panties, is how she controls me."
Dang, from the outside it looked like
'cool and the gang'.
So then at his new woman's house he started to hang.
But I couldn't get with that plan.
I decided to be a better 'All True Man'.

When I had urges to seek another lover,
I would hold up my son and say, "not to his mother."
My brother
that is 8 years older
thought that I could side step this stage
and see further from standing on his shoulder.
I told him I had been bitten
but couldn't find the serum.
"Sean, there are many snakes posing as women,
their poison comes from the inside
and nothin' can cure 'em"

Ain't that a trip?
I'm the number one mack, wit' a setback.
'cause I thought if I loved a little, gave a little,
struggled some and saved a little,
things would gravitate toward me,
move toward a pure destiny -
infinitely.

But she, couldn't keep our toxic relationship a secret.
We, went before a white guy in a black robe,
having no honor, but named "your honor",
and said, "How do you see it?"
"Remember your paycheck? Well you can't keep it."
Now see, her account increased in amount by half
before I could sign my check stub with my autograph,
I saw her and her new man begin to laugh.
To him I'm sucker number one -
paying for half her new car, half her rent,
I just got paid and half way home
my half of my paycheck was spent.
I said, "homeboy, you don't know the half
of what your laugh is about."
He continued.
So I got rid of half my rage and
half my anger
by knocking him completely
out.
Then I felt completely better,
except I noticed that when he fell,

he dirtied up one of my sweaters.
Anyway,
shortly after, I got a letter
from an old flame, with a familiar name,
that claimed, she could do better
if I could just believe and just let her.
But at this point I'm scared
to put even mustard and ketchup together.
It must have been the convincing song she sung.
She left out all the words
but remembered to flick her tongue
and It was so great till she went from
being a date, to a roommate.
Wait!
I never did
volunteer to cook, clean and keep her kids
while she stayed out late
and frequented the club.
Remembering,
this is why I'm sick of
                          Intoxicating Love.

GRASSROOTS
Rhythmic Travels of the Soul

REAL INTIMACY

I want to taste your mocha skin,
wash your hair and sprinkle fresh rose petals
in your bath water,

watch the flicker
of candlelight
bounce and dance in your eyes,

watch you grip my mattress
and bury your face in my pillow,

give you a manicure, pedicure, strawberry facial
and soothing vanilla hot oil body rub
after a hard day,

buy you elegant sexy clothes
that I would enjoy taking off slowly,

suck your sweet tongue, kiss your navel
and take off your panties with my teeth,

go to the theater and make out in the balcony
go home and have whipped cream fights,

stroke a feather across the back of your neck,
behind your knee, ear and small of your back,

serenade you with monotone moans
bodies in rhythm making our own love songs,

flick my eyelash against your cheek,
inhale the same breath you exhaled
lay breast to chest
and synchronize heartbeats

tickle your ribs with my beard and
nibble your inner thighs,

usher you into warm whirlpools on cool nights

making small ripples amidst the steam,

watch the sun come up together
after an overnight outdoor picnic,

feed birds and converse with zoo animals
as our ancestors once did,

leave poems on your windshield,
candy on your pillow,
and spray our names on a bridge,

kiss on the roof of a tall building
overlooking all that is ours,

hold your hand and glide it across
textures, etchings, sculptures and sketches,

fall asleep in your lap,
awaken in your arms

fix your favorite dish,
spoon feed you when you're sick,
hold your hand and laugh in the sunshine,
following trails of fulfillment,

and cry together
for those who have never found real intimacy.

EXHIBIT A

she took a chance
and I had plans in advance
to enhance
and clear up our previous love circumstance

and now
I like how
we find what's divine
combine and intertwine

reflecting what you feel when I express
you're an angel in low flight
when you descend
then
I am blessed

with a gift from heaven
in the form of a smile
a modern goddess
from your crown(hair)
to the ground
but with more attitude than the Nile

opposing any forces against your man
while remembering it's your divinity
that defeats the enemy
without raising a hand
assisting each child, in finding their smile
even, in their uneven situations
While some see it as merely raising a kid
you call it "building a nation"
and choose to nurture
by nature
teach through testimony
using energy to build
then recharge with your head on my chest
while you're resting on me

so when life throws us a barrage

and when reality really is a mirage
we don't collapse, we expand
and
turn this into a beautiful black collage

while others have a love
as frail as blown glass is
you set up my canvas(paper) and brush(pen)
and say "Sean continue painting pictures in the ears
of the masses"

and when some throw stones
slander and cause confrontations
you catch their dilemmas quick
form them into a brick
to further build our situation

And if there is ever a question
of love from me and to what degree
baby
I want to go to the Atlantic Ocean
and tell every fish in the sea
go underground and tell everything beneath me
I would go to outer space
just so I could carve it in the moon
of how I want to fall in love each July
and have it last until each June
because I would need to live 9 long lives
and use the ink from the pen
of every born scribe
to begin to tell you
how much I do

so much until
it must be a crime
so I charge you with
first degree love
premeditated kindness
and I must say
you crept inside my mind
until your thoughts too have become mine

so now
in this your trial
I wish to submit my love as Exhibit A

GRASSROOTS
Rhythmic Travels of the Soul

GRASSROOTS PART II (DEEPLY ROOTED)

We, the Grassroots remember blowout kits
and picking our naturals with that plastic,
black-fisted comb.
We watched 'Black-Belt Jones'
from the balcony at the Cameo Theater,
and later did the moves on our little brothers
to see which ones were real.

The Grassroots remembered to save a hug
for Big Momma, despite being scared
of her mustache and beard.

We used the living room
to form a soul train line,
and practiced 'The Temptation Walk'
in a full length mirror.

The Grassroots went to drive-ins,
took their own popcorn
in a brown paper bag
with oil and butter spots on it,
and sprayed 'Off' repellent
until their nostrils burned.

We watched 'Shaft go to Africa,'
unfolded the Isaac Hayes 'Black Moses' album cover
and tried to "keep our heads above water"
while James Evans lost
job after job after job

We borrowed the Duce and a Quarter
for those special dates,
and wore turtle necks
or body suits
with our favorite pair of bell bottoms.

The Grassroots slam-dunked
in their Chuck Taylor Converse All Stars

with three pair of socks on,
keeping the ankle weights from rubbing.

We were singin' "slippin' into darkness,"
and sippin' Thunderbird,
What's the word?
"Thunderbird."
What's the price?
"30 cents twice."
Who drinks the most?
"Colored folks."

Grassroots still flinch when thinkin' about
gettin' whipped with extension cords,
ironing cords, tree branch switches, leather belts
and hot wheels racing tracks.

We asked for another nickel
for extra milk money,
had to make another hole so
our watches and belts would fit

We spoke to the T.V. telling Dr. J.
to, "go left, go right, now finger-roll"
and witnessed the first slam dunk
from the free throw line.

We were proud when Ali beat Liston
and refused to go to war,
when the brothers
gave the black power fist at the Olympics,
when King opposed Vietnam, and when Richard Pryor
came from Africa saying he "saw no n-ggas
only beautiful black people," vowing with him to never
use that word again.

We played
Spades – Po keno - Bingo – Dominoes-
Bid and Rummy like a religion.

Now, we talk to 'Grandmaw' and 'Pops'

the way Fred Sanford talked to Elizabeth.

We have had rent checks to bounce
phones disconnected, showered with cold water
and even been fired from minimum wage jobs.

We wore Zips, Pro Wings, Pro Keds and Puma
before shoe contracts, and can still to this day
shoot a sweet fade-away and do a mean sky hook
despite laughs from the youngsters,
'cause they never knew nothin' bout Jo Jo White,
Tiny Archibald, Keith Wilkes and Lew Alcindor.

We used to pull taffy and "trick or treat" door to door
and never had to check the candy.
We listened for our names to be called at the
end of Romper Room,
Now I see...
Rode Huffy 5 speeds with sissy bars on back
of the banana seat, Western Flyer 10 speeds
and Evel Knievel dirt bikes
with an ace of spades strapped to the spoke
for a motor sound effect and vice grips firmly
around the seat neck for any roadside repairs.

We shot rubber band guns, sling shots
and Daisy Special B.B. guns.
Marbles were for keeps, and you could tell those
serious 'Jacks' players because of the scuffed outside
palm of their pick-up hand.

The Grassroots have won 350 cars
while playing The Price Is Right
nearly 2 million dollars on shows such as
Name That Tune, Let's Make A Deal, Wheel Of Fortune
and Joker's Wild but still must be 15 minutes
early to catch the Metro bus to work

We are versed in great literary works and compare

Manchild In The Promised Land, to Soul On Ice and Makes Me Wanna Holler

Our shelves hold Chester Himes, Ishmael Reed, Richard Wright and Dick Gregory next to Terry McMillan's and Eric Jerome Dickey's classics.

The Grassroots make it to work
with the gas hand on the red part,
put in $3 on the way home,
and chance our luck again tomorrow.

Our first pets were
a cat named Felix
a mutt named Underdog
and a Mighty Mouse.

We listened to bootleg tapes,
watched bootleg cable T.V.
and got bootleg liquor from The Bottoms on Sunday.

"Cotton comes to Harlem" was a prelude to crack

We were in love with Foxy Brown, Jayne Kennedy
Thelma Evans and Get Christy Love
and still pick up Jet Magazine and turn
straight to page 43 to check out the
Beauty of the Week.
We "spill some" for the brothers who ain't here
and play the dozens
and slap-box with the ones that are.

We raced Popsicle sticks in the gutters
after the rain and played "That's My Car."

We snapped our fingers to applaud
when Maya, Gwendolyn and Sonja recited
and tapped our toes when Ray, B.B., Wes and Miles played.

Without the Grassroots,

nothing, absolutely nothing, could prosper or grow.

We have been analyzed, but never defined,
only labeled -
as "those colorful,
grassroots people
with Soul!"

GRASSROOTS
Rhythmic Travels of the Soul

WE!!! HE???

He is always the late one
to the gym
no one really knows him

He is always
wearing lipstick
and the guys wonder
if they should shower
or if he will get the nerve
to ask
for their phone number

He is always wearing lipstick
and I bet he drives
a little car with
a rainbow on the bumper
he probably wears those little shorts
and claims to be a 10k runner

This guy who always wears
this trace of lipstick
should be kicked out of
the Men's locker room
we're betting on whether
he wears panties
or Fruit of the Loom
should we call him out
or will he be coming out soon

If this guy in the dark red lipstick
had asked
We guys, "the single five"
would have given him
one or maybe even two
of our girlfriend's friends
fornication maybe be wrong
but
He chose the bigger sin
looks like we can never be friends

since he likes a soprano's song
and has a broken wrist
as oppose to a tight fist
we can't invite him along
to the game or the big fight
because we call it "Guy's Night"
and by the way
who respects the friend
of someone gay
then
suddenly all of the guys in the gym
look his way
then three small children
come over and say
"Hey daddy I hope you have a good day"
as he anoints their foreheads
with a kiss
as this
attractive lady says "Honey, you forgot this"
giving him his gym bag
containing his watch, wedding ring, and keys
then he whispers "Thanks baby and
can I have another one of these?"
As we hold down our heads
and unclench our fists
His wife smudges his mouth
with dark red lipstick
as she gives him a kiss ☺

BOYS LIKE ME

Her kisses linger
after I pluck them
from amid the clouds
I hover between
the two soft curved pillars
that hold up my heaven
Both anxious and surreal
grown men shouldn't feel... like this
unless, their youth
never truly dies...
unless, pulling on pig tails
is just traded for
nape of the neck caresses
and heart warming compliments
unless, shy fumbling gestures
mimic coordinated fondling
unless, coy winks
grow up
to become full fledged gazes
or vice-versa
No not unless our once juvenile
taste buds
begin to prefer
"Sugar and spice, and everything...
naughty"

Previously we existed
by going from one mirage
to the next mirage
and now finally
from
a mirage to our marriage

Grown men that feel
like this
still value our
basketball card collections
and eat cereal
during Saturday morning cartoons

while the gravity of our ladies
both holds and elevates us
Yes, it's easy to notice
Boys Like Me since
our girls may still have
pigtails or ponytails
but more importantly
She is water
to our spirit
and We
can be found
skimming across the earth
walking
with buoyancy

EYES OF AN ANGEL

The eyes of an angel
the birth of a soul
this pleasure beyond measure
in our arms, daily watching and helping you grow

Your focus is unfixed
Your optic nerve is still weak
to notice what this world has to offer
both bitter and cold, welcoming and sweet

To give you a world
better than it is now
to be the parents that the creator intended
so you can continue your heavenly smile

Your birth came with a glow,
it brightened my most sunny day
Excuse me for mumbling this English language
I understand
your "baby talk" is closer to what angels convey

The smell of my newborn
is sweeter than any perfume known to man,
the feeling of closeness that overcomes me
when I stick out my finger
and you grip it with your little hand

Kissing chubby cheeks and tickling tiny feet,
No other joy can compare
to this near 10 pounds of perfection
when into your angel eyes I stare

GRASSROOTS
Rhythmic Travels of the Soul

GRANDMAW'S HANDS (FOR IDA MOONEY)

Grandmaw's hands,
tender enough to catch me
before a fall,
rugged enough to till and reap
next year's crops- Grandmaw's hands.

Grandmaw's hands,
callused from washin' on the wash board,
could outdo Maytag.
Like John Henry,
NO machine beats Grandmaw's hands.

Grandmaw's hands
worked in blistering summers
and bone chilling winters,
for me, you, us and them other folks
but never solely for Grandmaw.

Her hands had thick veins
underneath her shiny leather skin.
They must have formed a map to and through
The Underground Railroad.
Each scar and scrape told and showed
the love for her people,
just looking at Grandmaw's hands.

No sculptured or Lee press-ons,
just thick unmanicured nails
with fingerprints
that must have been left on some ol' axe
or plow.
A lot of milk came from a cow
by the pull of Grandmaw's hands.

No need for gold or tennis bracelets,
her skin
out shined any diamond or gem.
Soul from her foot tap
to her hand clap,

enhancing and living the words
of the old Negro spirituals and gospel hymns.
Her fingers floated across
the piano
her sweet voice followed
in a feathery falsetto, a velvety soprano

My Grandmaw cooked
everything from scratch
so we didn't eat out a lot.
Others could make the same dish
but I swear hers was delicious,
I think she must have had the love in her heart
drip from her hands
down into the supper pot.

My hand in Grandmaw's hand
made me feel so secure
And how I wish she was here
so I could feel the pure
embrace of warmth and love
of my dear
Grandmaw's hands.

CONQUERABLE SOUL

My eyes leak tears
tears that burn trails down my cheeks
searing holes in my pillow
and inside
my heart has calcified
water is symbolic of energy
so understandably
tears from agony
leave me with a tainted chi

I'm beyond return
and wasn't given a bridge to burn
somewhere beneath grief
below low
can't go
or, let go
motionless, or at best, slow
no room to grow
defeat has conquered
my unconquerable soul

The "right road"
I would choose
but my beliefs are bruised
lack of
"I love you"
has me highly explosive
with a short fuse
from once confident and compassionate
to now combustible and confused

So 'Failure' must be my name
I hope you never feel the same
listening to my heart
over my brain
regardless if it's
a sham or just a shame
I'm to blame
out of quarters

love is the hearts gamble
love is an unfair game

Lesson
It sometimes takes an entire village
to destroy a boy
but a single woman can deploy
a plan to extinguish a grown man's joy
especially if she is to be his wife.
Death,
is having no control over life
and breathing
becomes optional
I never believed it possible
to drown one raindrop at a time
but looking up at MY clouds
I now see
for me
it may be
probable

So now I,
form into a fetus or fist
when I cry
remembering when I refused to let go
heaven knows
you have just witnessed
the death
of my once optimistic soul

A MACK GONE GOOD (SEAN'S REFORMATION)

Hey pretty girl
let's make a caramel and chocolate swirl
supreme
and can I entice you into auditioning
for the role of My Queen
take our time, as our spirits align
with our bodies becoming
so in tuned
until our screams will break glass
and our minds will bend spoons
I'm not talking all night
I'm talking more like
From now until next June
flip the calendar and then
it will be so good until
you'll have to go call your girlfriend
rip up your little black book
of all your ex-men
and when you want some more dear
just come over here
because
"I only stopped, so we can start all over again"
shoot, I wish you had a twin
but not so I could cheat or creep
but so you could take over her existence
and I could fall in love with you again
you see
Teena Marie
was left "Out on a limb"
but you can come in
to some love as gentle as a dove
and kisses from lips
with feathers in them
and hugs possessing the strength
of 50 or more strong men
you see
I want to hold you like
a Siamese holds his twin
like how a wine-o

holds his gin
like how a writer
holds his pen
or like how the pen
holds our black men
some say that love is a game
if so, I want you to know
that I play to win
and if you can catch these lyrics
that I'm throwing to you
it should get us a first and ten
but not so I can just cross
your physical goal line
it's known that $E = mc2$
was given to the world by Einstein
but the equation that you came
and put on my mind
is that
cute plus sexy, equals fine
and
I bet that after all of this time
you think that I've been talking about sex
but...
what I really want to do
is
make love to your mind

TO BE CONTINUED...

IF YOU CAN COUNT YOUR MONEY
(a poetic rap song)

You like the way that the
platinum shines
extracted spines
on women that are fine
you said no to a model
that was a 9.9
stressin' the fact that
you only got time for dimes

payin' for homeboys' funerals
and postin' their bail
Movado watches with imported diamonds
bought at wholesale

you went from drivin' a Benz
to buyin' your crew Bentleys
went from singles and fives
to hundreds and fifties
stackin' only new big faces
that are still sticky and crispy

reading The Robb Report
no more Donald Goins
investing in
rare gold coins
resting in
exclusive clubs where thugs can't join

involved in
high speed chases
and the look on cops faces
when the sergeant escorts you home
because
he's on your pay list

a casino Gambino
with matching diamonds
in your ear and your cuff

winning on a bluff
walking away leaving two grand on the table
'cause it
wasn't enough

you got a personal barber
to keep your hair in a fade
bought your butler a Navigator
and a 'Vette for your maid
and your house you say
"it's just okay"
with indoor full court to play
and original art
on display in the hallway
you got a chandelier
with 10,000 candle watts
to turn the night into day
nice enough to make projects
look like caves
you change cars with the days
Lexus jeeps on Mondays
and antique Stingrays on Tuesdays
and Wednesdays it's custom Bentleys
Thursdays it's Q45 Infinity
Friday it's the Benz 600
and Saturday it's the Jag and the Nav
for the big crew
that you run with
trying to rest on Sunday
from all your play
with seven parked cars in front of your beach house
with heated circle driveways
six master bedrooms because
you don't believe in slaves

whirlpool baths
his and hers nozzles in the same shower
Australian crystals
sprinkled in your kids' Wittenauer
living plush
as we discuss

how life is tough
for us struggling blacks
while your car plays
CD's
DVD's, mp3's
and DAT's
bulletproof, with tires that
can run on flats
and instead of shotgun
kids fight to sit in the back
where the video games are at

your lifestyle's abundant
future billionaires you run wit'
play spin the bottle with fine wine
from the 1800's

because only a few
have true wealth
while others be out here fakin' it
but if you see me
without money
it's because they stopped makin' it

we went from
bus passes
to passin' busses in Maserati's
to leather floors
covered with Flokati's
from riding wheelies on Kawasaki's
to cruising on Ducati's

Lambo's and Peugo's
with that remote control starter ignition
our cars TVs are plasma screens
with that high definition
so stop look and listen
my throat is a clutch
and my tongue does the shiftin'
No drink, No reefer
my poetry sounds sweeter

when you adjust your bass and tweeter
from a Carver receiver
Nakamichi CD
into a Bose speaker

my vocals flex
to bring in big time checks
from big execs
got big body guards
that take out all the haters and haterettes
they jump in front of Glocks and Tech's
and be like, "Who's next to test?"

you see they
sacrifice their lives
for us to have our fun
because
like Don King said
"If you can count your money,
then you ain't got none"

This is Sean Tyler the poet
spillin' the real
saying consider what you love and like
because it just might
get you killed

BETWEEN THE NUMBERED SHEETS

My poetical rhymes
are known from time to time
to start off innocent and inky
and end up kinda kinky
the pages become the sheets
the binding serves as covers,
we're more than just friends
see me and my girl "Pen"
are more like secret lovers

We're serious at times
and sometimes we "do it" for fun,
regardless,
it's always euphoric bliss
since
me and my Pen always come...
to a point

And when your hand is on the page
you too are engaged
since in reading
you borrow the writers freedom,
and know that when
you get the urge again
you can join me and my Pen
but realize
you just made it a threesome ☺

GRASSROOTS
Rhythmic Travels of the Soul

SIMPLE COMPLEXITY

She
loved me
in spoonfuls
yet I thirsted for gallons
the challenge
was not to meet my satisfaction
but to keep me anticipating
and reacting
while knowing
to give what I'm asking
only enhances my multi-tasking

The initial loving action
is always a simple solution
for such a complex infraction

GRASSROOTS
Rhythmic Travels of the Soul

NO ONE

I just gave birth
to a beautiful verse
but no one noticed it
but me.
In an empty forest
who hears falling trees?
Is there an instrument
that captures the sounds
of the wind moving leaves?
Who can guess
which tiny wave
drives the motion of the sea?
In one day,
how many people recognize
the amount of air they breathe?
And
who even cares about
my broken heart
and forfeited dreams?
No one.
No one, but me.

GRASSROOTS
Rhythmic Travels of the Soul

MOURNING DEW

It's a slow silent sunrise
and I'm slipping into a robe
as my mind slips into images
you left behind.
Today is a perfect day for lovers.
But my forecast
is mental overcast,
resulting in cloudy gray eyes,
which yesterday brought about precipitation
in the form of tears.
The scattered moisture reappears
on eager and lonely
days like today.

GRASSROOTS
Rhythmic Travels of the Soul

HOW GOOD INTENTIONS DIE

Her words went from
rose petals to razor blades
cutting my dreams short
causing my ambitions to bleed
and stain the floor
of my honest intentions

a goddess
with a gun for a tongue
aimed at my heart
ejecting hollow points and views
in an automatic delivery
we
didn't make the news
but we did die
cut and wounded miserably

GRASSROOTS
Rhythmic Travels of the Soul

WEDDING DAY BLISS (A LETTER TO MY BRIDE)

Angel,
  Looking into your eyes reminds me
of how you make me feel like a child again
in that I always get butterflies
when we hold hands
and become light-headed
shortly, after we kiss

  When you're away
I become anxious
as if it were Christmas Eve
and when you're near
your warm smiles
seem to melt, my childish worries... away
I then feel as if all of my
birthday and first-star wishes
have finally, come true

  The kid in me
wants to return your glass slipper
and serenade you
in hopes that you come down from your balcony
while the grown man in me
is eager,
Eager to marry you, Today
and then continue to,
date you, forever

  I want us to delight
in each moment together
even beyond,
when we will someday
trade-in our sneakers for walking canes
beyond the time when
our wrinkled hands
secure our wedding rings

  I want to learn from you

and grow with you
and ask you to marry me
Again and Again, every ten years

   Angel, I promise to help you to become
the kind of woman that our future daughters
should aspire to be
and the model in which our sons
should later seek, and cling to
A woman in whom God
will be well pleased

   I will not forget to cherish you,
love and protect you
as any man should
once he finally, finds
his life's treasure

   I promise to be kind, gentle
and to listen
to listen each day
to the music
We have composed in our hearts
and
in each others Lives

I LOVE YOU- ST

THE CALM AFTER MY STORMS (ME AT 35)

I am no longer lonely
in my aloneness
my self-pity has been used all up
and bursting from underneath
my shortcomings labeled
ego, hatred, anger and fear
I found faith
A faith that is detached from
a self absorbed expectation
absent of the desire to control
or change another

My faith is the opposite of my fear
it fosters perfect kindness
which truly and completely
frees me
As I forgive and ask forgiveness
I make room in my life for miracles
I strive to be everyone's positive reflection
Today,
I am
love
in
motion

GRASSROOTS
Rhythmic Travels of the Soul

Thanks to my parents Luther and Inaclaire Brown, and Franklin Tyler, aunt Sylvia, uncle Harry, my brothers and sisters, nieces and nephews. extended family, the Block family and my friends.

Thanks to the mighty B.P.C. and its associates, Mrs. Wright, Nimrod, Louis, Gino, Tara, Tony, Ted, Kuma, Breeze, Wilson, Natasha, Kenan, Kre-8, Glenn, Myron and Stacy.

Thanks to O.B. Kamau, Charles Berry and Lloyd Daniel for inspiring me to want to write.

Thanks to Kimberly Hines, Larry Hill and Dr. Deloris Pinkard for EVERYTHING!

Thanks to Fermon Byers, Brion Dennis and Carlos Burdine for unconditional friendship.

A special thanks to my smart and beautiful wife Angel and my strong and handsome son Ahmad, I Love you both

GRASSROOTS
Rhythmic Travels of the Soul

Please feel free to share your comments and thoughts about Grassroots with me. I will try to respond to everyone promptly. www.Grassroots777@aol.com (Sean P. Tyler)

S.P.T.- PEACE AND UNITY